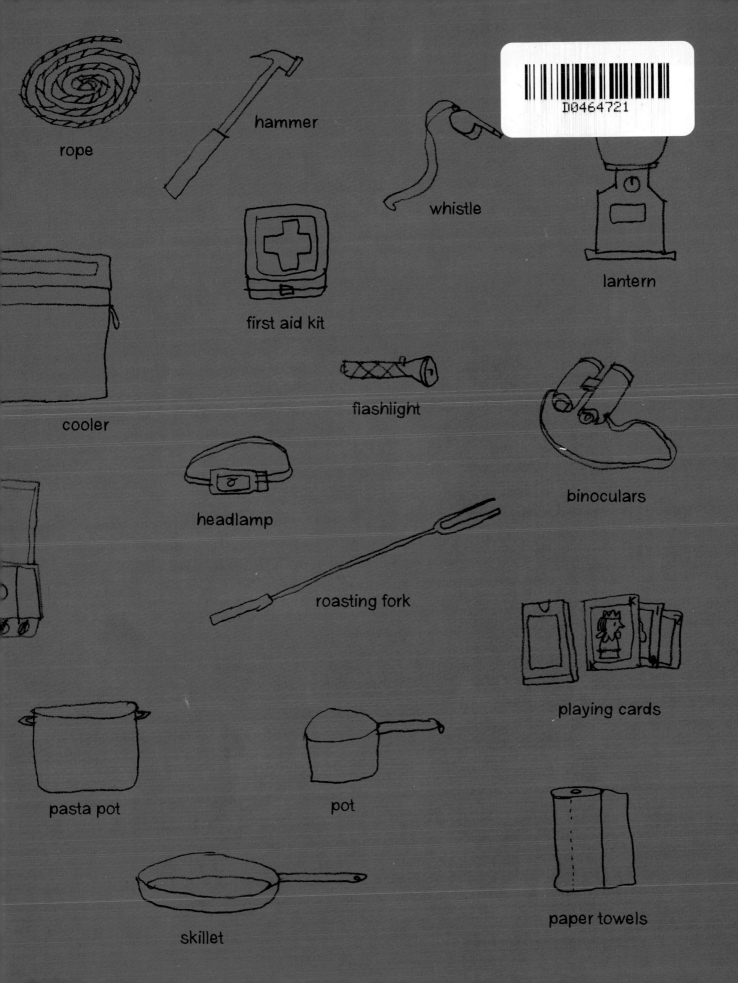

rope

hammer

whistle

lantern

first aid kit

cooler

flashlight

binoculars

headlamp

roasting fork

playing cards

pasta pot

pot

skillet

paper towels

This book is dedicated with love to
Anna, Curren, Eliza, Than, and their parents.
Thank you for all the unforgettable camping
memories already made, and those yet to come.

First edition 2020

Library of Congress Catalog Card Number pending
ISBN 978-1-5362-0736-1

20 21 22 23 24 25 CCP 10 9 8 7 6 5 4 3 2 1

Printed in Shenzhen, Guangdong, China

This book was typeset in Archer and AnkeSans.
The illustrations were done in pencil on tracing paper,
then digitally collaged and painted.

Candlewick Press
99 Dover Street
Somerville, Massachusetts 02144

visit us at www.candlewick.com

# THE CAMPING TRIP

Jennifer K. Mann

CANDLEWICK PRESS

MY AUNT JACKIE invited me to go camping with her and my cousin Samantha this weekend, and my dad said yes!

I've never been camping before, but I know I will love it.

I got a sleeping bag . . .

and a new flashlight!

And Dad and I made some trail mix, just for camping.

Aunt Jackie sent a list of things to pack:

hat

sneakers

flashlight

water bottle

backpack

towel

pajamas

camera

sleeping bag

pillow

sunblock

underwear

swimsuit

shorts

Foxy

sunglasses

bandages

T-shirt

sweatshirt

swim masK

socks

comic books

whistle

trail mix

It's a long drive to Cedar Tree Campground.

We look at comic books.

We play cat's cradle.

We stare out the window.

We sing along with the radio.

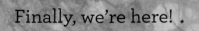

Finally, we're here! .

It's so quiet. And big.
It smells like trees, and fire,
and dirt.

You need a lot of stuff to go camping, so it takes a long time to unpack.

Samantha and I decide to set up the tent. I build forts all the time at home, so this should be easy.

It's not one bit easy.

I'm sweating.

Me too!

Let's swim.

OK.

I love swimming at the Y.
I can touch the bottom
of the pool!

When Samantha is finally done swimming, we eat lunch.

My dad says hiking is just walking—but in nature instead of in the city—and I walk to school every day.

Here's what I need
to go hiking:

backpack
hat
sunglasses
whistle
camera
water bottle
sunblock
granola bar
trail mix
apple
raisins
leftover chips
cheese sticks
peanut butter crackers
cookies
bandages
Foxy

There are a lot more hills here
than on my way to school.

My feet are tired already.

Maybe I brought too much stuff.

I think I need a water break.

When we finally stop, I eat a lot so my backpack will be lighter on the way back!

It's way easier to hike downhill.

When we get back to the campsite, Samantha and I set up the campfire.

What's for dinner?

Tofu hot dogs and broccoli salad— my favorites!

This is what you need for s'mores:

marshmallow

graham crackers

chocolate

a marshmallow–roasting fork

Mine is perfect!

Mine's on fire!

First you roast your marshmallow over a campfire.

Then you make a sandwich.

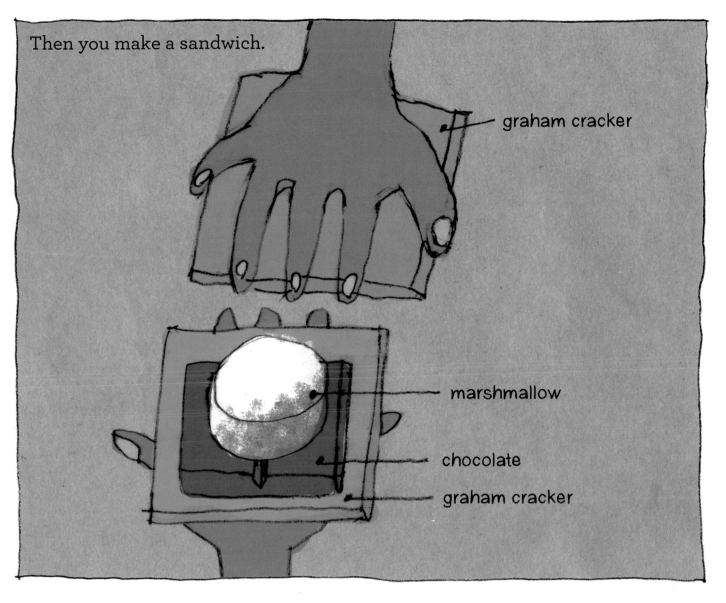

graham cracker

marshmallow

chocolate

graham cracker

And then you eat it. S'mores *are* scrumptious!

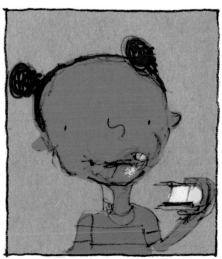

I crawl into my sleeping bag, and we read with light from
Aunt Jackie's lantern until she says it's time to sleep.

Two seconds later, Aunt Jackie and Samantha are snoring. But I can't sleep.

I'm boiling.    I need to get my socks off!    Where's my water bottle?

  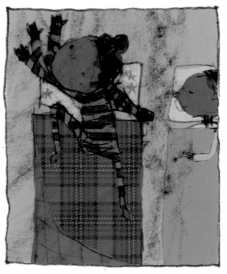

Where is Foxy?    I'm freezing.    Is anyone else awake?

Is Dad awake?

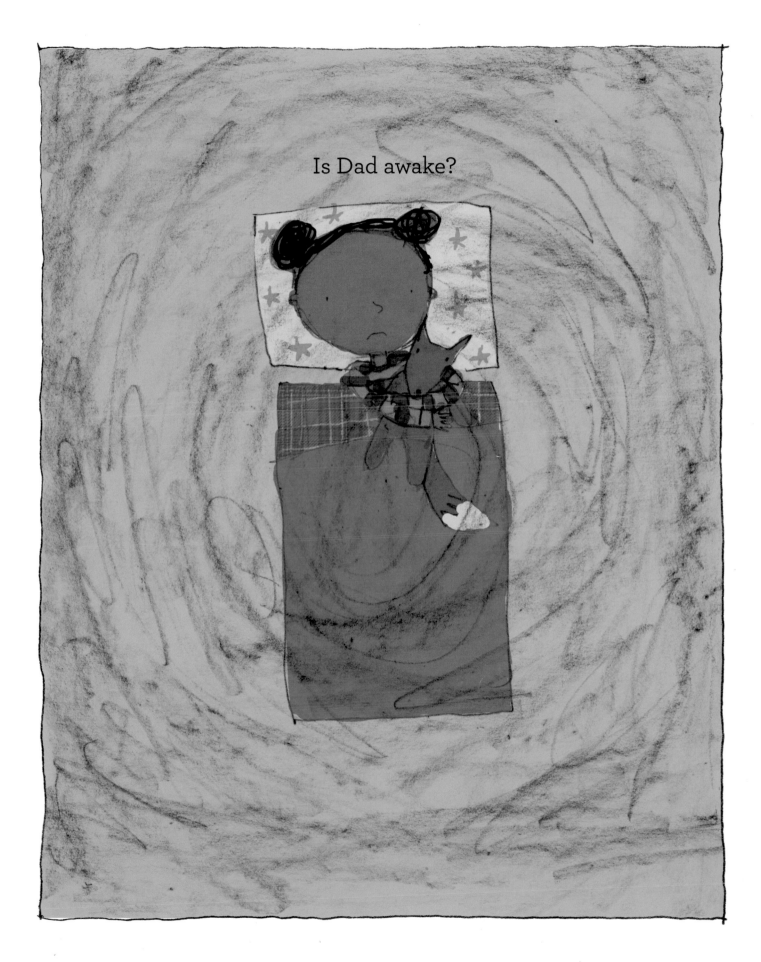

Aunt Jackie lets me use her phone, but there is no reception.

It's really dark.

When I wake up in the morning,
the tent is warm and bright.

Aunt Jackie and Samantha
are already eating breakfast.

These are the best pancakes ever!

Packing up is even harder than unpacking.

When we finally get our stuff in the car,
it takes all three of us to close the back.

Goodbye, Cedar Tree Campground! I can't wait to come back next year.
Me too!

It's a long drive back home.

We eat the rest of the trail mix.

We stare out the window.

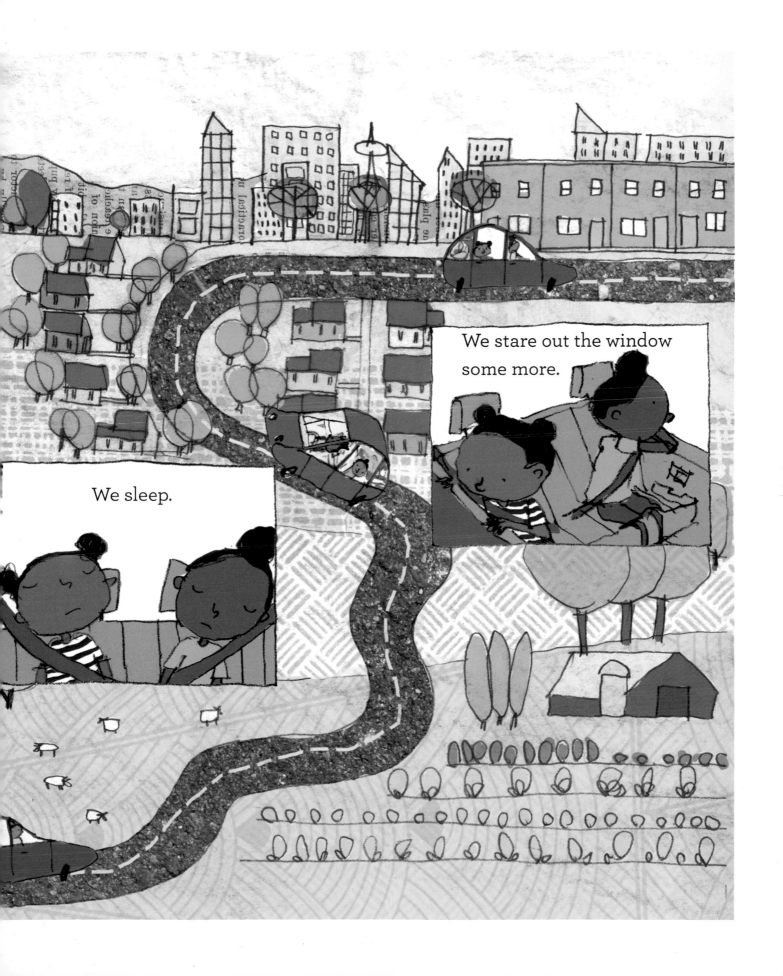

We stare out the window some more.

We sleep.

I think Dad missed me.

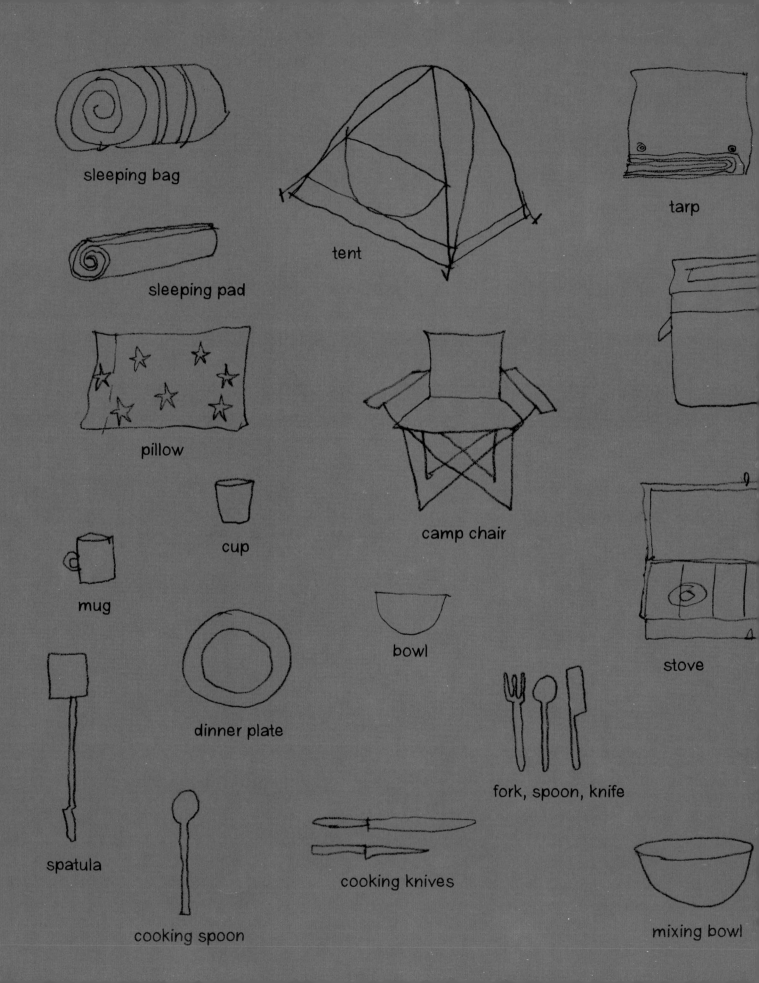

sleeping bag

sleeping pad

tent

tarp

pillow

camp chair

cup

mug

bowl

stove

dinner plate

fork, spoon, knife

spatula

cooking knives

cooking spoon

mixing bowl